DINOSAUR SCIENTISTS

Nicolas Brasch

Australia • Brazil • Japan • Korea • Mexico • Singapore • Spain • United Kingdom • United States

Dinosaur Scientists

Text: Nicolas Brasch
Editor: Ben Haskin
Design: James Lowe
Series design: James Lowe
Photo researcher: Corrina Tauschke
Production controllers: Lisa Porter and Renee Cusmano
Reprint: Siew Han Ong

Acknowledgements
The author and publisher would like to acknowledge permission to reproduce material from the following sources:
AAP Image/Dave Hunt: p. 9; Alamy/Peter Casolino: p. 16; Alamy/Phil Degginger: p. 21 (top right); AP Photo/Rick Rycroft: p. 22; Corbis/Annie Griffiths Belt: pp. 4–5 (inset); Corbis/Layne Kennedy: p. 5 (main); Corbis/Louie Psihoyos: pp. 13, 21 (centre left); Corbis/Paul A. Souders: p. 19 (top); Corbis/Richard T. Nowitz: p. 11; Corbis/Xinhua/Xinhua Photo: p. 15 (bottom); Corbis Sygma/Pitchal Frederic: p. 17 (top); Corbis Sygma/Vo Trung Dung: p. 17 (bottom); Getty Images: pp. 3, 4 (main), 10 (main), 20, back cover; National Geographic Stock/IRA BLOCK: p. 21 (bottom right); National Geographic Stock/Kenneth Garrett: p. 10 (inset); National Geographic Stock/O. Louis Mazzatenta: p. 8; National Geographic Stock/Sam Abell: p. 14; Penguin Books Ltd – front cover of *The Lost World* by Arthur Conan Doyle (Puffin Books, 1994), cover copyright © Penguin Books Ltd, 1994: p. 23 (inset); Photolibrary/Highlights for Children: pp. 6–7; Photolibrary/JML: p. 19 (bottom); Photolibrary/Pat Canova: pp. 1, cover; Photolibrary/Philippe Plailly/SPL: p. 12; Photolibrary/Photo Researchers: p. 15 (top); Richard Morden © Cengage Learning Australia: p. 18; Shutterstock/Bob Ainsworth: pp. 4–5 (background), 8–9 (background), 14–17 (background), 20–21 (background); Shutterstock/Chen Ping Hung: p. 9 (background); Shutterstock/Peter Jochems: p. 9 (notebook); The Kobal Collection/Amblin/Universal: p. 23 (main).

Every effort has been made to trace and acknowledge copyright. However, if any infringement has occurred, the publishers tender their apologies and invite the copyright holders to contact them.

Fast Forward Independent Texts
Level 13

For product information and technology assistance,
in Australia call 1300 790 853;
in New Zealand call 0508 635 766

For permission to use material from this text or product,
please email **aust.permissions@cengage.com**

ISBN 978 0 17 017979 9
ISBN 978 0 17 017897 6 (set)

Cengage Learning Australia
Level 7, 80 Dorcas Street
South Melbourne, Victoria Australia 3205

Cengage Learning New Zealand
Unit 4B Rosedale Office Park
331 Rosedale Road, Albany, North Shore NZ 0632

For learning solutions, visit **cengage.com.au**

Printed in Australia by Ligare Pty Ltd
3 4 5 6 7 2 22 21 20

Nicolas Brasch

Contents

Finding Out About Dinosaurs

Scientists who find out about dinosaurs are called palaeontologists.

Palaeontologists have been able to find out a lot about dinosaurs, by looking at **fossils**.

Fossils, which are found in rocks, are what is left of plants and animals from a very long time ago.

fossilised insects and spider

Looking at fossils helps palaeontologists find out how the dinosaurs lived. Palaeontologists can find out where and when the dinosaurs lived, and what they ate.

The work of palaeontologists helps people to imagine the world when dinosaurs lived on Earth.

Fossils also help palaeontologists find out what Earth was like millions of years ago.

Becoming a Palaeontologist

It takes a long time to become a palaeontologist.
Fossils are found in rocks,
so people who want to be palaeontologists
need to learn about how rock layers form.

Case Study

Scott Hocknull: palaeontologist

Scott Hocknull was only eight
when he started to like dinosaurs.

From the age of 15,
he helped out on **digs**
with the Queensland Museum.

Scott studied science
at the University of Queensland.

He got a job as a palaeontologist
at the Queensland Museum
when he was only 22.

CHAPTER 3

Working as a Palaeontologist

Palaeontologists go to places where they think there could be fossils.

Fossils are often buried a long way under the ground.

using ***technology*** to find fossils

Palaeontologists have to dig up the fossils,
which can take a long time.
So they often work in teams,
and stay at a dig for weeks.

Palaeontologists take any fossils they find back to **museums**, where they clean them and look at them very closely.

Museums are not just for showing things from the past.
They also have places to store and fix things.
There are places to work and teach, too.

Tools of the Trade

Palaeontologists use many different tools. They use heavy machines to dig down to where fossils are.

Palaeontologists use shovels to dig up fossils without breaking them.

Picks and **brushes** are used to get rid of dirt and rock from around the fossils.

Back at the museum,
palaeontologists take a very close look
at the fossils,
using special tools to make them
look much bigger.

Palaeontologists use special technology to look inside fossils.

This machine can take very detailed pictures of the inside of fossils.

Palaeontologists use Earth's rock layers to guess the age of fossils. The deeper rock layers are older than the top layers.

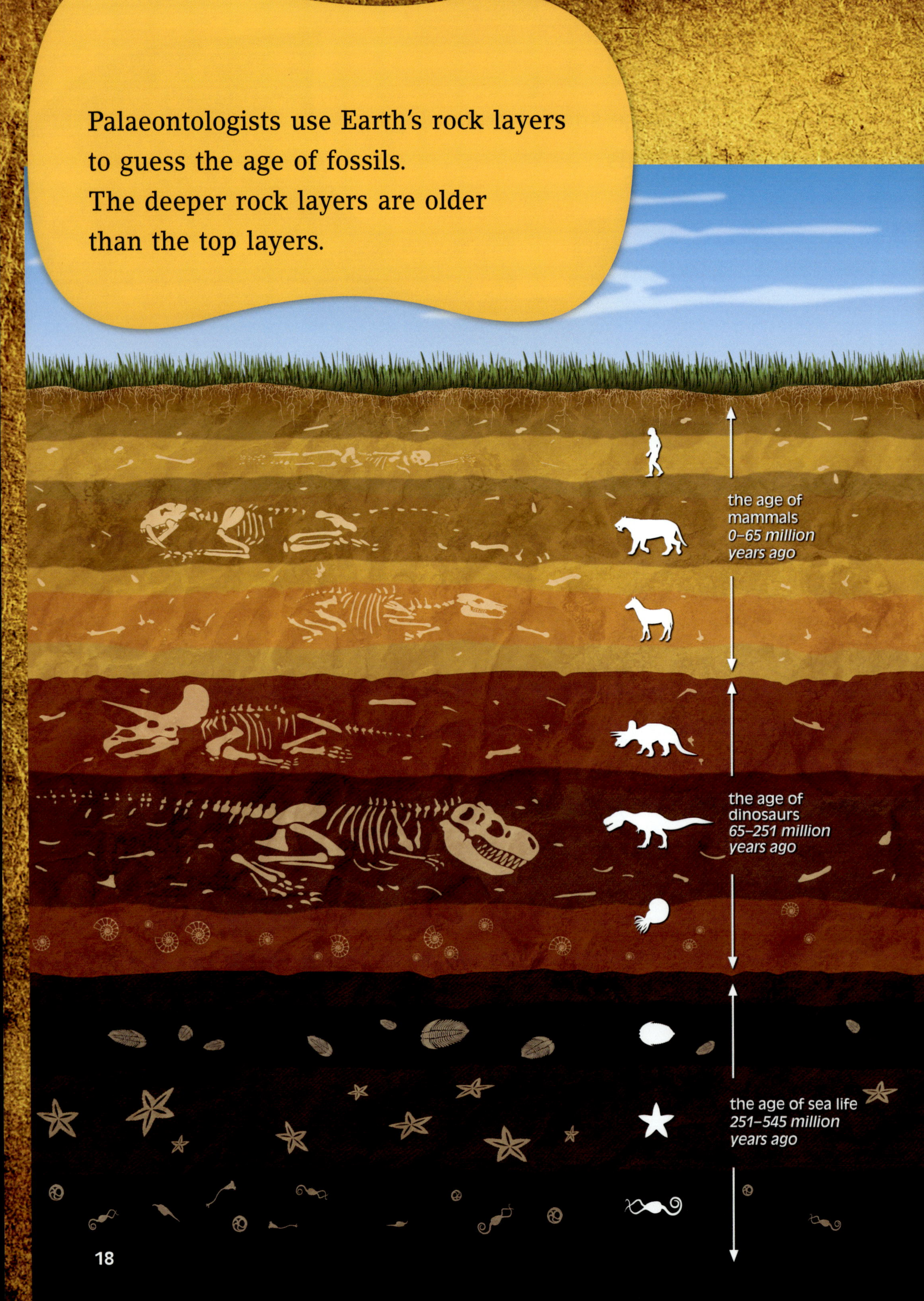

A fossil is about the same age as the rock layer that it is found in.

Palaeontologists also use special technology to find out how old fossils are.

This machine is used to find out the age of a fossil.

CHAPTER 5

Dinosaurs on Earth

Dinosaurs lived on Earth
for about 180 million years.
They lived on Earth
from 245 million years ago
until 65 million years ago.

Hundreds of different kinds of dinosaur fossils
have been found all over the world.
There may still be many more
to be discovered.

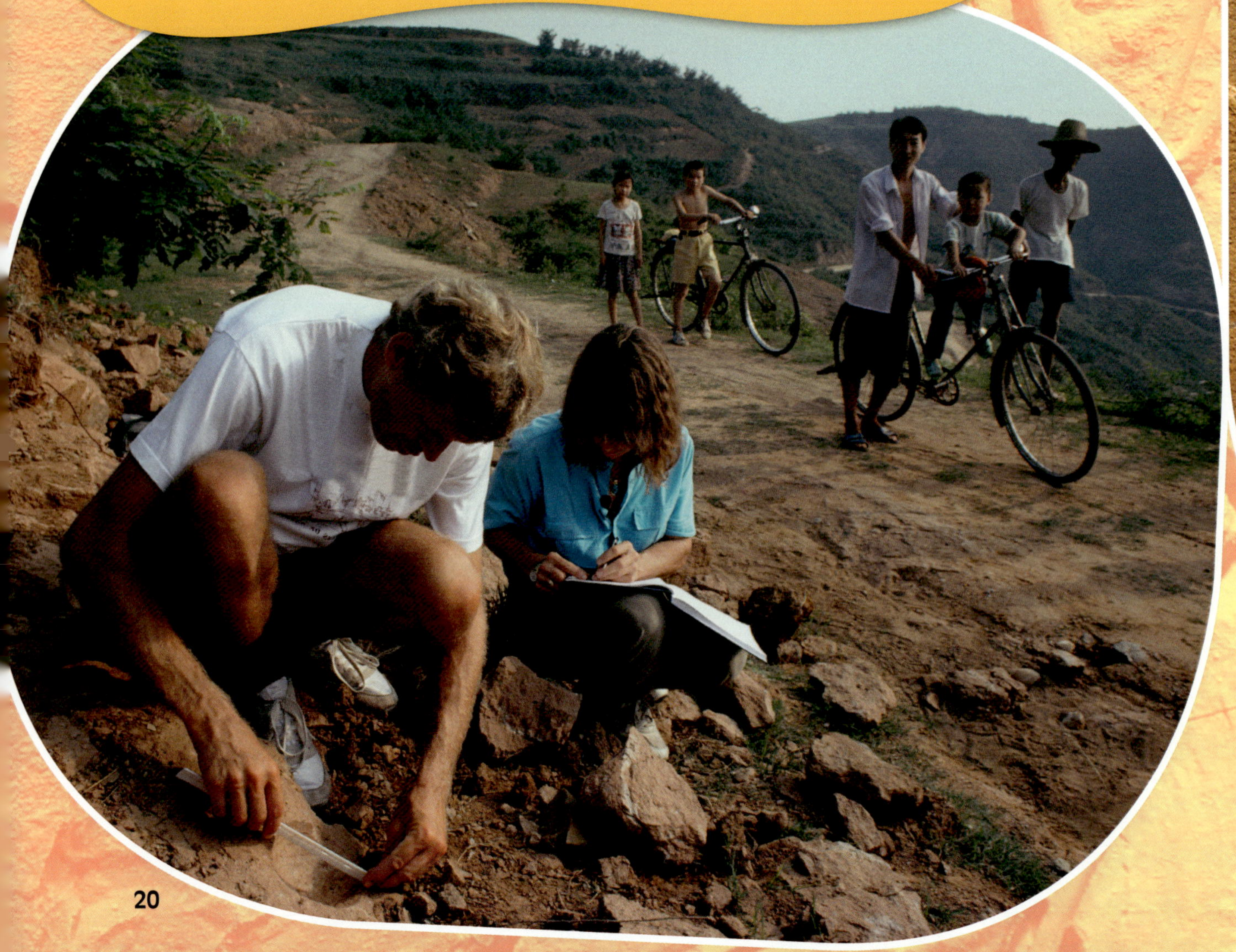

a Triceratops *skull*

a fossilised prehistoric bird

a Tyrannosaurus rex *skull*

Seeing a Real Dinosaur

The work of palaeontologists helps people think about what it would be like to see a real dinosaur.

a scene from the film Jurassic Park

Books and movies about dinosaurs have become very popular. Even though dinosaurs are extinct, these stories give them a new life.

Glossary

brushes tools with bristles attached to a handle, used for getting rid of dirt from fossils

digs sites where palaeontologists dig up fossils

fossils the remains or tracks of living things from long ago, hardened into rock

museums places where valuable and interesting things are studied, looked after and shown

technology scientific tools

Index